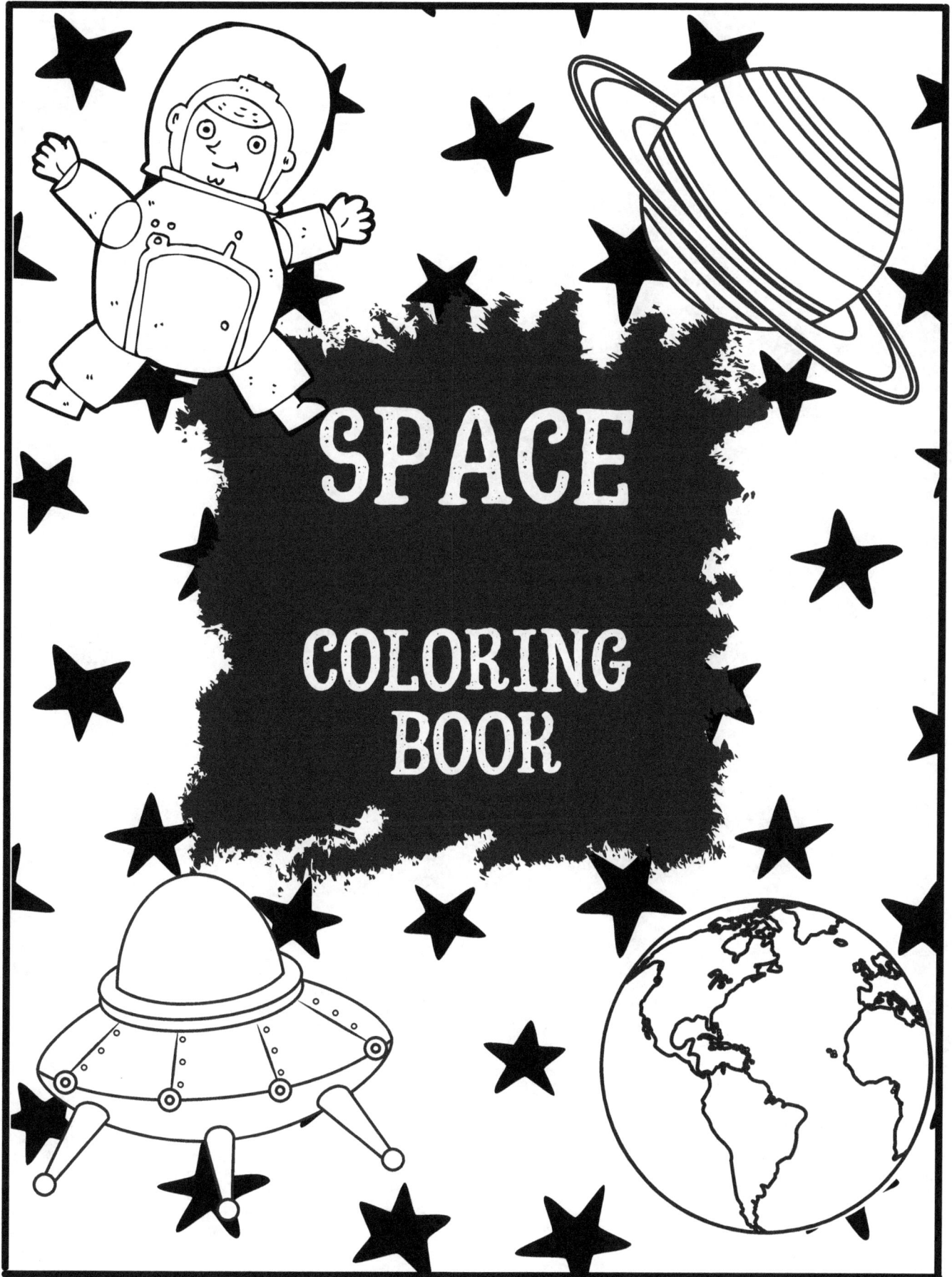

SPACE

COLORING BOOK

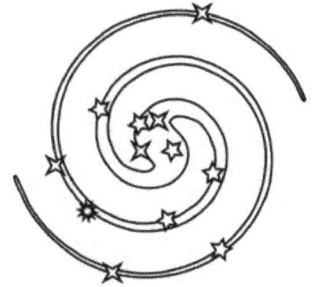

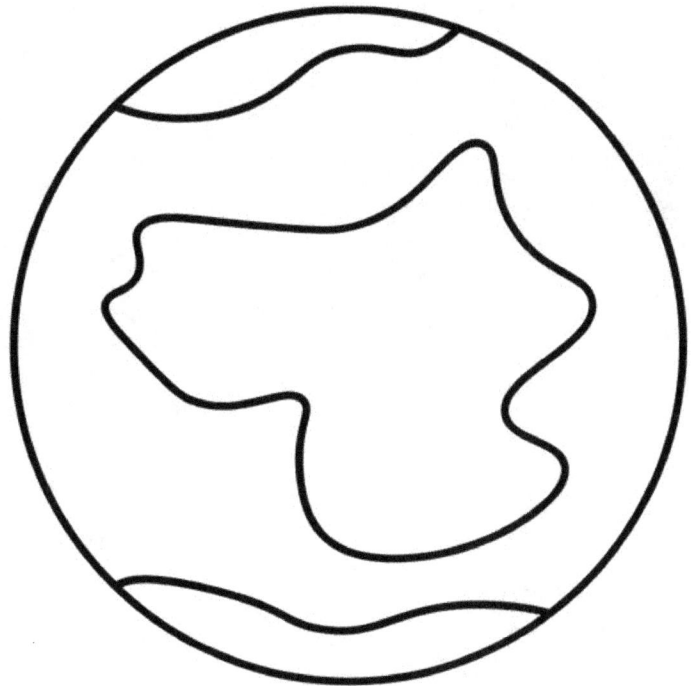

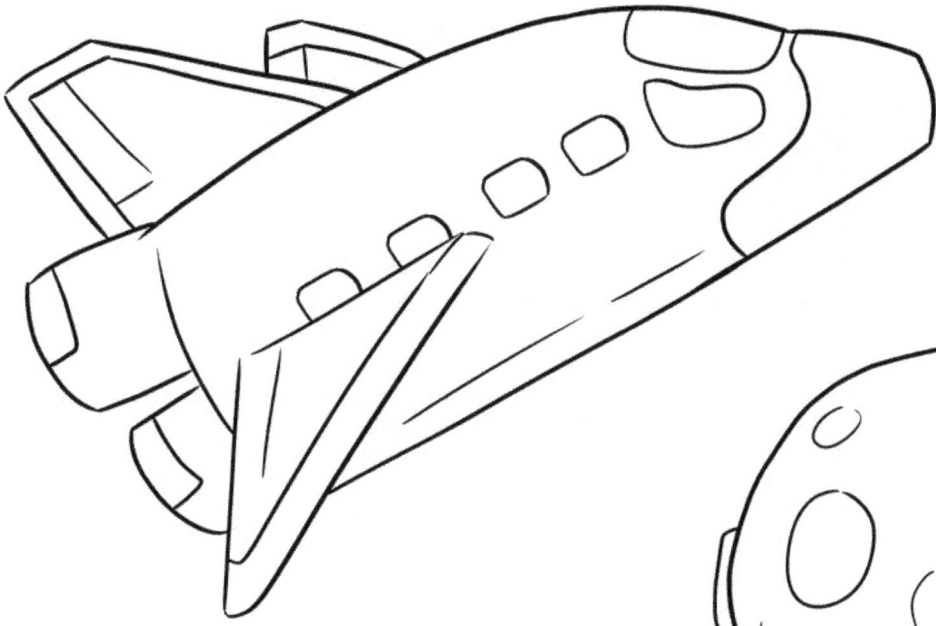

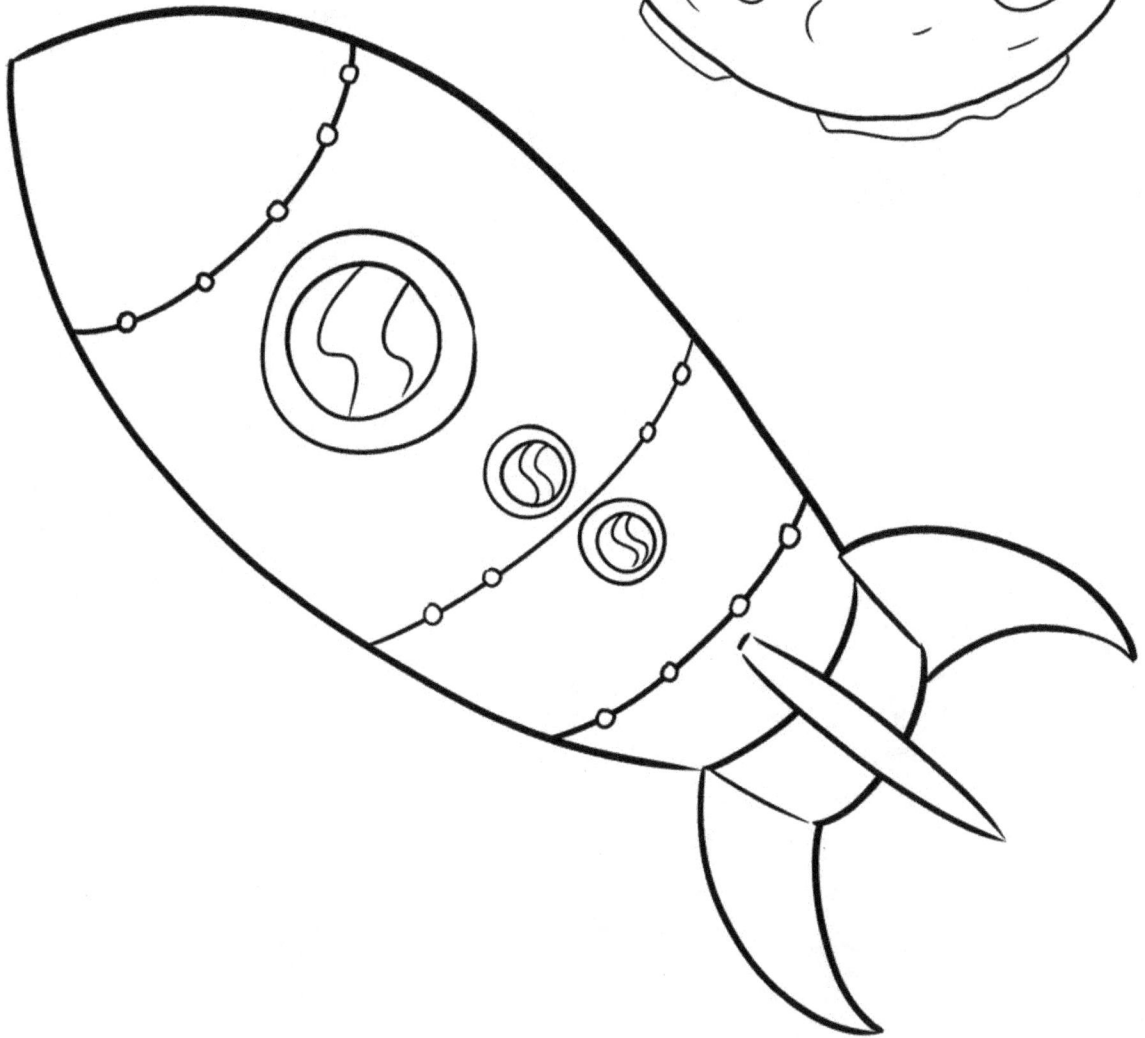

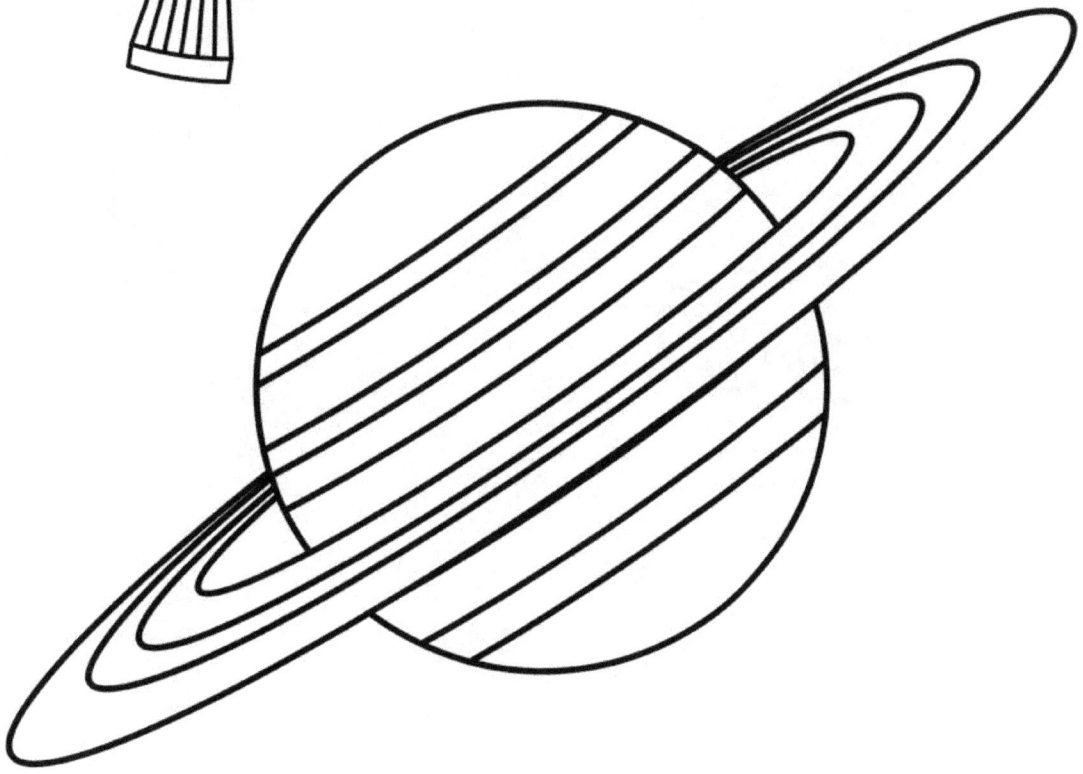

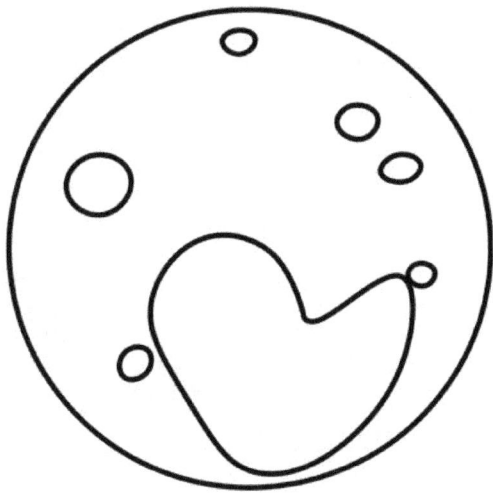

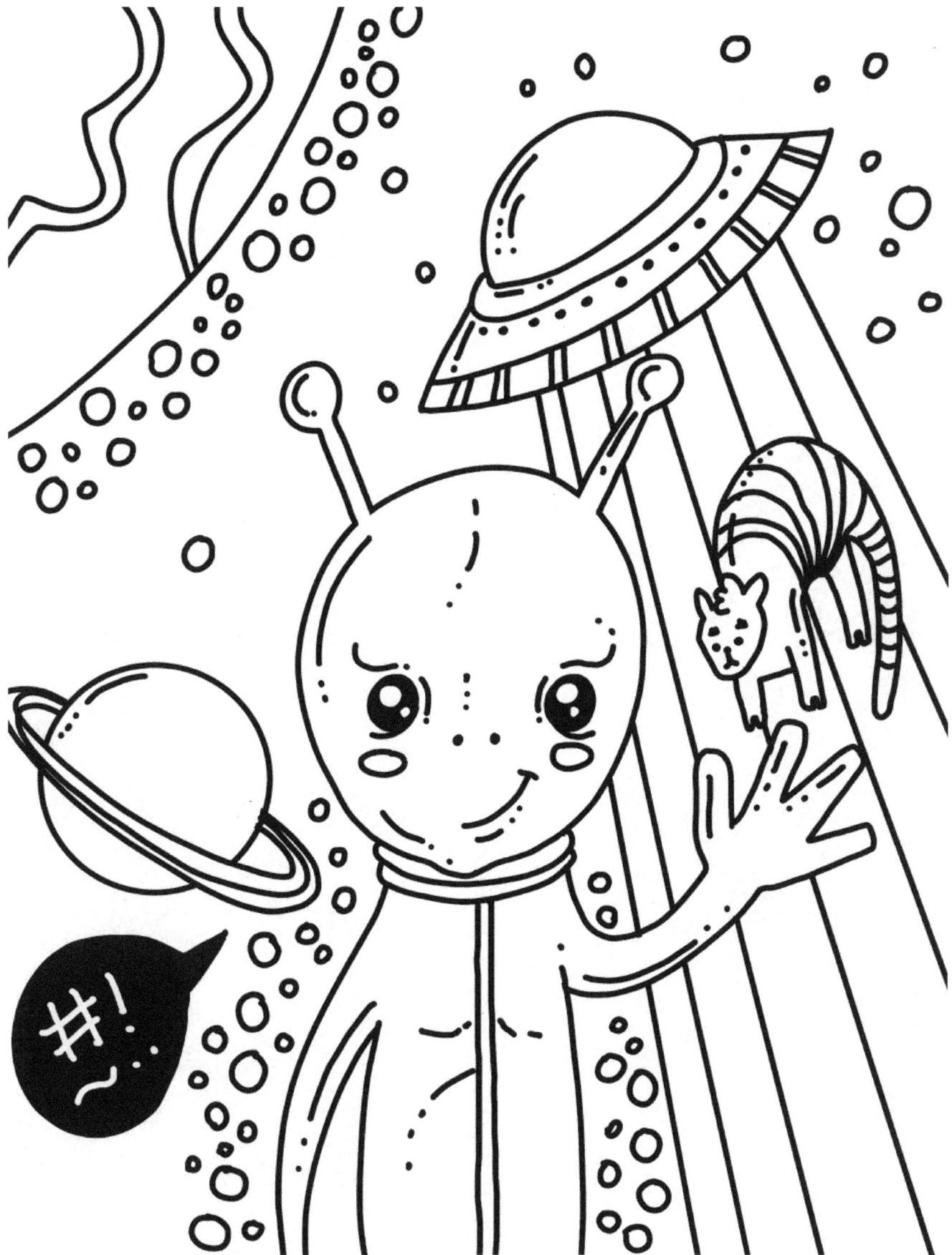

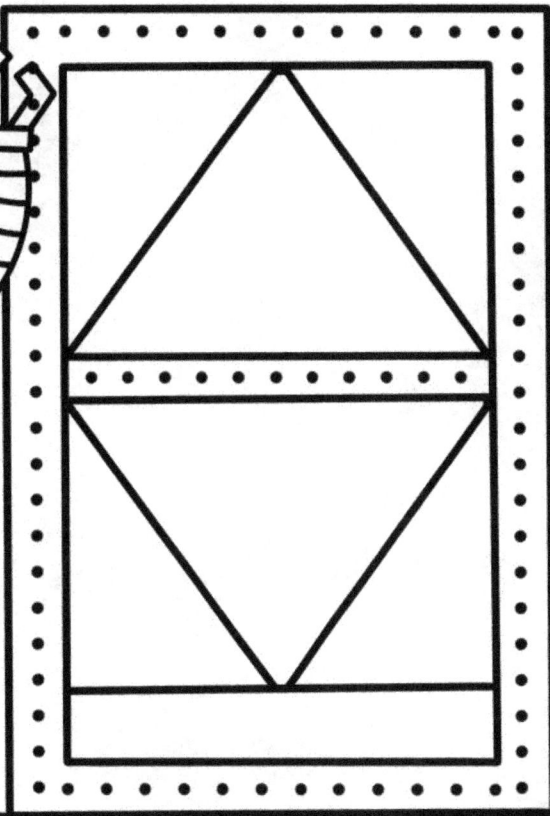

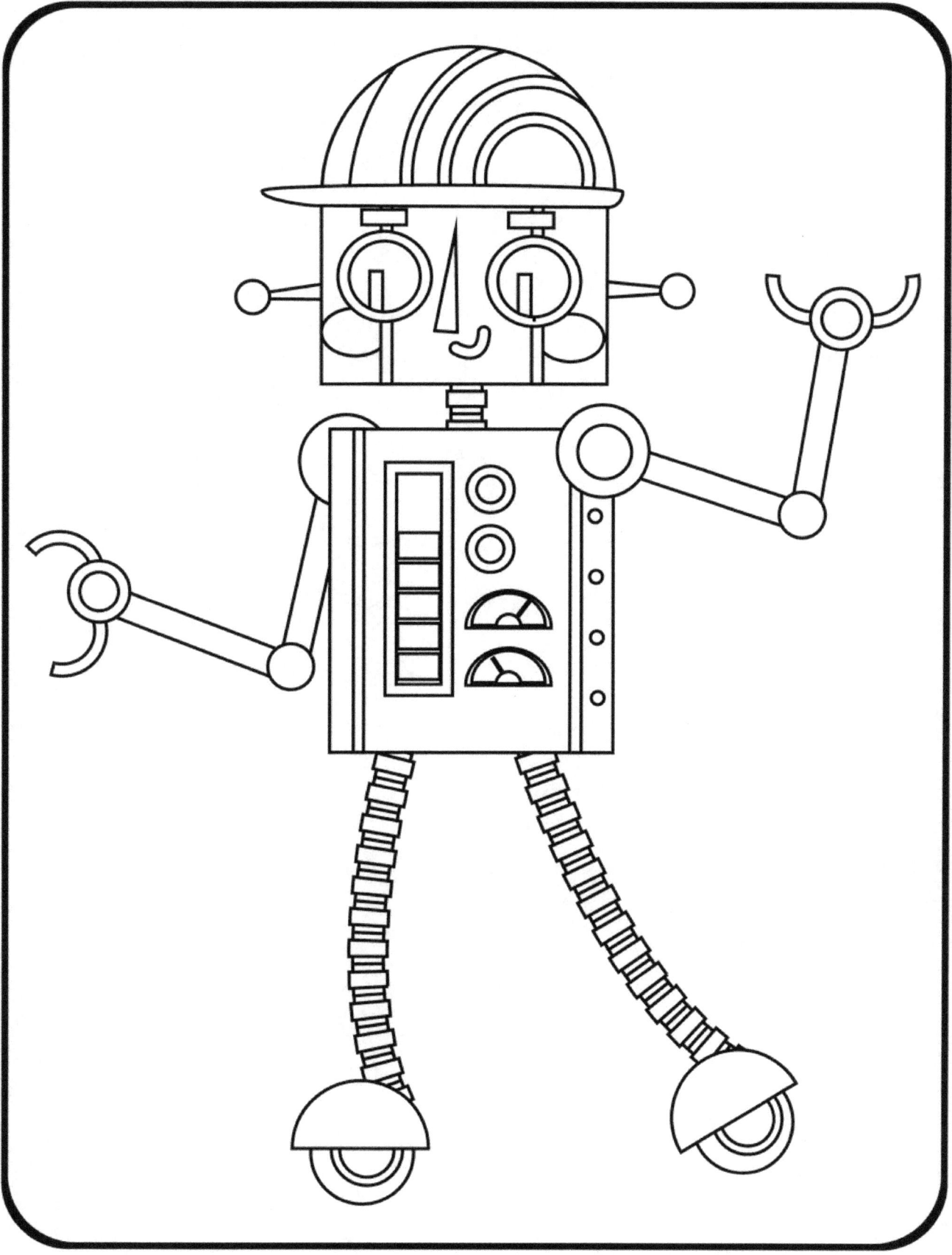

SPACE

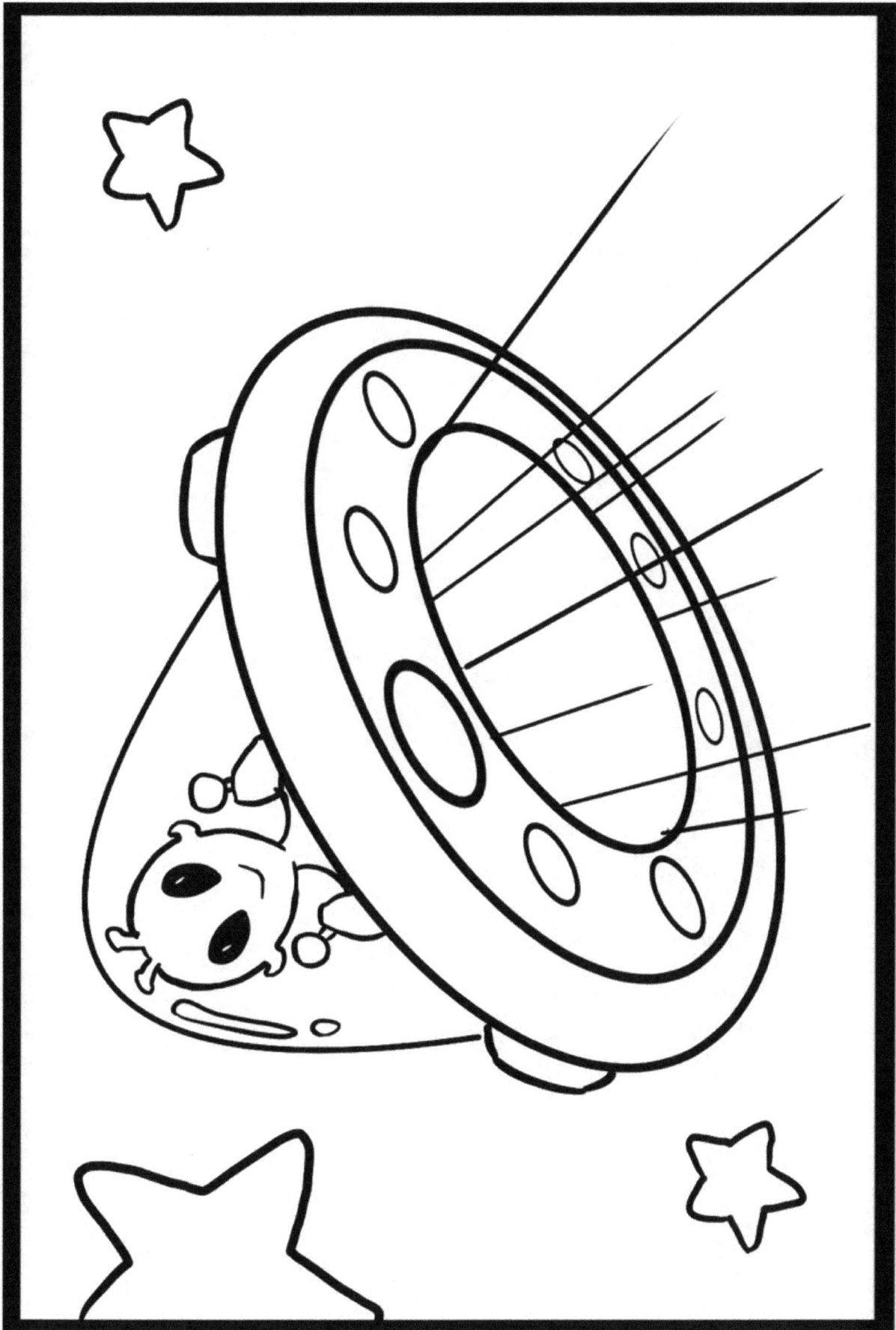

Thank you!

We hope you enjoyed our book.

As a small family company, your feedback is very important to us.

Please let us know how you like our book at:

wallstersbookshelf@gmail.com

f Wallster's Book Shelf

○ @wallstersbookshelf

CPSIA information can be obtained
at www.ICGtesting.com
Printed in the USA
BVHW010850170521
607540BV00003B/101